# Bunny Loves to Read

First published by Parragon in 2011

Parragon
Chartist House
15-17 Trim Street
Bath BA1 1HA, UK
www.parragon.com

Written by Peter Bently
Illustrated by Deborah Melmon
Designed by Rachael Fisher
Edited by Rachel Worgan
Production by Richard Wheeler

ISBN 978-1-4454-5801-4

Printed in China

# Bunny ♥♥ Loves to Read

PaRragon

Bath • New York • Singapore • Hong Kong • Cologne • Delhi
Melbourne • Amsterdam • Johannesburg • Auckland • Shenzhen

Buster Bunny loved books.

He read stories of princes...

and pirates...

and witches and wizards...

One day, Buster's friends came over.
"Hi Buster!" they said. "Are you coming
out to play?"
"Sure," said Buster with a smile, "when I've
finished my book. It's all about pirates!"

"You've always got your nose in a book!" said his sister Bella.

"HOpscOtch is much more fun!"

"Books are boring!" croaked Francine.

"Why read books when you can play leapfrog?"

"Reading is not as much fun as racing each other," agreed Max.

"Don't listen to them, Buster," said Sam.
"I think books are the best!"
"Really?" asked Buster.
"Yes," said Sam, smiling. "Books *are* the best –

Then Bella said, "Come on, let's leave Buster with his dumb old books and play outside!"

But it was raining.
The friends looked out
the window gloomily.

"Why don't you read
some of my books?"
asked Buster, bringing
out a big box.
"We don't want to
look at books," said
Sam grumpily. "We're
only waiting for the
rain to stop."

Buster took a book out of the box.
"There's a big thunderstorm
in this story," said Buster. "It's all
about pirates hunting for buried
treasure."

"Buried treasure?" asked Sam.
"Like nuts and acorns? Yum!"

"Not exactly,"
replied Buster.
"But it's very exciting.
Take a look."
"I guess there's nothing
better to do," sighed Sam.

"Frogs hate being stuck inside!" grumbled Francine.

"This book is about a prince who turns into a frog," Buster said.

"Good for him," said Francine. "Does he turn back into a prince?"

"Why don't you read it and find out?" smiled Buster.

"Being cooped up inside is making me sleepy," said Max.
Buster gave Max a book. "The princess in this story
goes to sleep for one hundred years!" he said.
"Really? WOW! How does she wake up?"
"Read it and see!" said Buster.
"Well, okay, but I might fall
asleep before I finish it!"

"I'm bored! I'm going to get a cookie," said Bella.
"Hey, Buster, your box is in my way!"
"Can't you just step over it?"
"Only if I take a giant step," said Bella.

"Just like a dinosaur!"
said Buster.
"Some of them were
**bigger** than a **house!**"

Buster looked out of the window.

"Hey, it's stopped raining!" he cried. "Who's coming out to play?"

Shh! I'm still reading. The pirates haven't found the treasure yet!

"So what do you want to play?" asked Buster when the friends had all finished reading. "Hopscotch? Leapfrog?"

"Let's pretend we can do magic spells. If you give me a kiss, I'll turn into a princess!" said Francine.

"Ugh! No thanks!" laughed Sam. "Let's play pirates!"

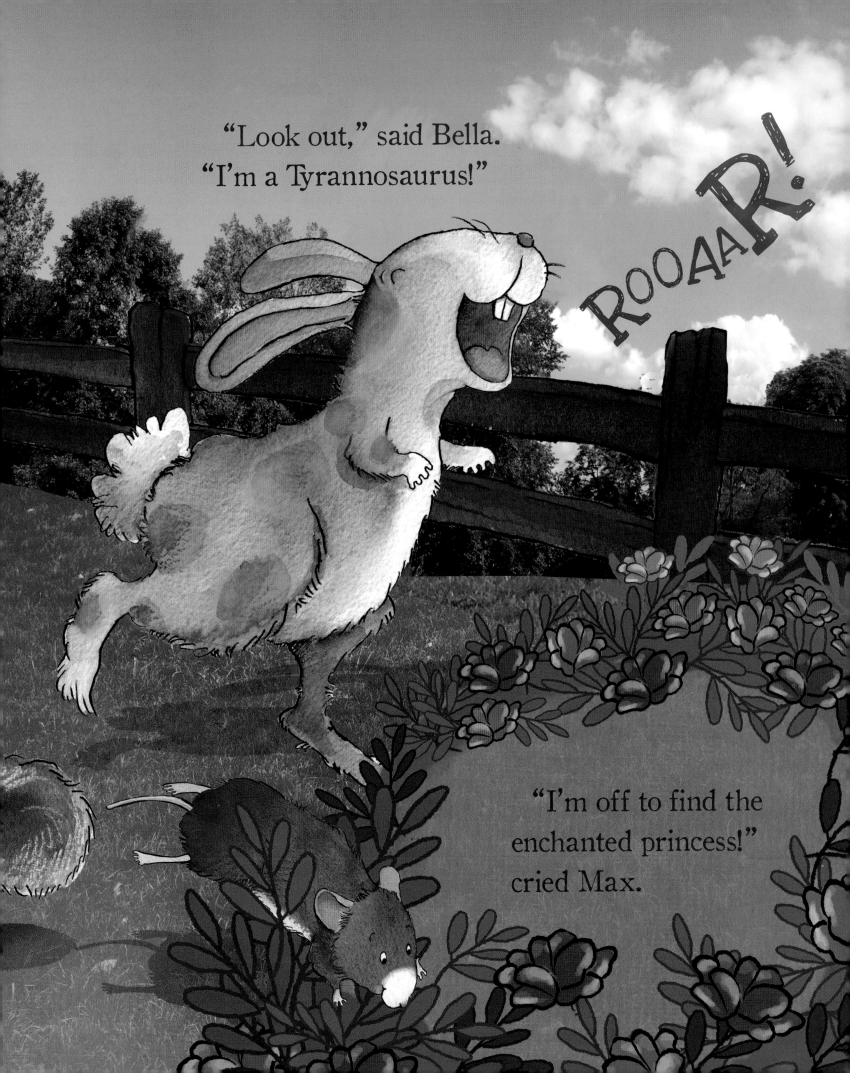

"Look out," said Bella.
"I'm a Tyrannosaurus!"

ROOAAR!

"I'm off to find the
enchanted princess!"
cried Max.

They played pirates and dinosaurs
and princes and princesses until it
was time to go home.

"Do you have any other books about dinosaurs?"
asked Bella.

"Sure!" said Buster.

"What about frogs?" asked Francine.

"Yes," said Buster. "And toads too."

"Anything else about witches and magic?"
asked Max.

"Lots!"

"Can I borrow another pirate story?"
Sam asked.
   "Of course you can,"
laughed Buster, "as long as you promise
not to eat it!"